OVERFISHING

By Therese Shea

Gareth Stevens
Publishing

Please visit our website, www.garethstevens.com. For a free color catalog of all our high-quality books, call toll free 1-800-542-2595 or fax 1-877-542-2596.

Library of Congress Cataloging-in-Publication Data

Shea, Therese.
Overfishing / by Therese Shea.
 p. cm. — (Habitat havoc)
Includes index.
ISBN 978-1-4824-3318-0 (pbk.)
ISBN 978-1-4824-3319-7 (6-pack)
ISBN 978-1-4339-9925-3 (library binding)
1. Overfishing — Juvenile literature. 2. Sustainable fisheries — Juvenile literature. I. Shea, Therese. II. Title.
SH329.O94 S54 2014
338.3727—dc23

First Edition

Published in 2014 by
Gareth Stevens Publishing
111 East 14th Street, Suite 349
New York, NY 10003

Copyright © 2014 Gareth Stevens Publishing

Designer: Andrea Davison-Bartolotta
Editor: Kristen Rajczak

Photo credits: Cover, pp. 1, 15, 27 Jeff Rotman/Peter Arnold/Getty Images; p. 4 Comstock/Thinkstock;
p. 5 Cecile Treal and Jean-Michel Ruiz/Dorling Kindersley/Getty Images; pp. 6, 8, 9, 14, 20 iStockphoto/
Thinkstock; p. 7 Franco Banfi/WaterFrame/Getty Images; p. 10 Beth Swanson/Shutterstock.com; p. 11 (main)
Ethan Daniels/Shutterstock.com; p. 11 (inset) Natali Glado/Shutterstock.com; p. 13 (main) Wayne Barrett
& Anne MacKay/All Canada Photos/Getty Images; p. 13 (inset) Globe Turner/Shutterstock.com; p. 17
Andreas Altenburger/Shutterstock.com; p. 18 Visuals Unlimited, Inc./Patrick Endres/Getty Images; p. 19
Paul Sutherland/National Geographic/Getty Images; p. 21 (both) Hemera/Thinkstock; p. 22 Ingram
Publishing/Thinkstock; p. 23 Alex Hofford/AFP/Getty Images; pp. 24, 25 courtesy of NOAA; p. 26
Tim Sloan/AFP/Getty Images; p. 29 Suzanne Kreiter/The Boston Globe via Getty Images.

Printed in the United States of America

CPSIA compliance information: Batch #CW14GS: For further information contact Gareth Stevens, New York, New York at 1-800-542-2595.

Contents

Words in the glossary appear in **bold** type the first time they are used in the text.

A WORLD WITHOUT FISH?

Overfishing is a pretty simple idea. It's catching more fish than can be replaced in a population through breeding. Enough fish must be left to grow, have offspring, and repopulate bodies of water. For many years, when fishermen used simple nets and fishing poles, overfishing wasn't too much of a worry. Today, because of **technology** and huge, profitable businesses, it's a great concern.

In fact, some scientists think disaster looms in the future if something doesn't change soon. They believe the present rate of fishing will exhaust all commercial **fisheries** by 2050!

Cold Fish

A hundred years ago, fishermen kept close to shore because they had to worry about their catch spoiling. Even an onboard compartment of ice would melt after a time. With the inventions of refrigerators and freezers, fishermen began to be able to stay out on the water for a longer period, catching more.

"Commercial fishery" is the term for an area where fish, shellfish, and **crustaceans** are caught to be sold to the public.

WHY YOU SHOULD CARE

You might wonder why overfishing is such a big deal. If all the tuna in the world were caught, you could never have another tuna fish sandwich or tuna roll at your neighborhood sushi restaurant. But there are other results, too.

Every living thing in the ocean is part of a food chain. If one link in the chain disappears, it harms the **habitat**. Tuna eat a lot to grow very large. They eat smaller fish, squid, crustaceans, and other sea creatures. If they died out, these animals' populations would explode. They, in turn, might eat too much of another kind of fish, causing them to disappear.

What About Farmed Fish?

Fish farms produce half of the seafood the world eats. That's still not enough to save the fish in our oceans. Unfortunately, some farms harm ocean habitats and even use wild fish as food, making the overfishing situation worse. Other farms are overpopulated, leading to unhealthy conditions. These fish farms, too, need to adopt better practices.

fish farm

The largest tuna ever caught was an Atlantic bluefin tuna, weighing 1,496 pounds (679 kg). Bluefin tuna are very hard to find in some places where they were once plentiful, such as the Mediterranean Sea.

TROUBLE IN THE CORAL REEF

Even if you don't like seafood, you should worry about overfishing. Killing too many of any sea creature causes problems beyond the food supply. For example, many fishermen catch sharks by accident. These sharks are then thrown back, wounded or dead. Twenty percent of all sharks are currently **endangered**, so these "accidents" make the problem worse. Even sharks are important members of their habitats.

Let's look at one kind of shark—the Caribbean coral reef shark. Scientists are discovering that coral reef sharks play an important role in keeping coral reef habitats healthy. As they disappear, the habitat suffers.

reef shark

All the sea creatures living on and around a coral reef depend on each other.

Coral Reefs

A coral is a tiny sea creature with a hard skeleton. Many corals join to form coral reefs. Reefs give fish, crustaceans, and other sea life hiding places from predators. Corals take in carbon dioxide to create their skeletons. Without corals, the amount of this gas would increase, negatively affecting all life in and out of the ocean.

Scientists believe that coral reefs with many predators at the top of their food chain are home to more kinds of sea creatures than those with fewer. Caribbean reef sharks are one of these top, or apex, predators. They prey on fish and crustaceans along the outer edges of coral reefs from Florida to Brazil.

So what happens if reef sharks disappear? The fish and creatures they eat would grow in population. In turn, the plant-eating fish that those animals consume would shrink in population. Then, there would be fewer fish to eat harmful **algae** and plants. The corals might die, and the habitat might be destroyed.

dead coral reef

From Reef to Table

Coral reefs are home to more than 4,000 kinds of fish, crustaceans, and shellfish, which feed between 30 and 40 million people every year. By protecting the sharks and other sea creatures that live in coral reefs, people are protecting the balance of nature there—and a huge food source. So far, more than 10 percent of reefs have been damaged beyond recovery.

dried shark fins

Some fishermen cut off sharks' fins and throw the sharks back in the water to die. Shark fins are used in a popular Asian soup.

KILLING THE COD INDUSTRY

The coast of Newfoundland was settled largely because of the profitable cod fishing in the North Atlantic. **Trawlers** and traps made it easier to catch northern cod in large quantities. Even when the cod population decreased, sonar and radar allowed fishermen to find the remaining cod.

In the 1970s, an international fishing organization put a maximum limit, or quota, on the number of cod that could be caught. However, it greatly **overestimated** the population. To make matters worse, some ships changed their flags to appear to be from nations that weren't involved in the quota agreements. Others used nets with smaller holes to catch younger and smaller fish.

Advances in Fishing

Sonar uses sound waves to pinpoint the position of underwater objects, while radar uses radio waves. Before these technologies, fishermen had to guess where fish could be found. Now, they know where fish are, how far down, how many, how fast they're swimming, and more.

At one time, Europe saw Newfoundland as more important than the whole of New England because of the fishing industry.

Newfoundland

Canada

United States

In 1992, less than 121,200 tons (110,000 mt) of cod were caught near Newfoundland, even with all the technology available to the fishermen. If this amount seems like a lot, consider that about 1.8 million tons (1.6 million mt) were caught in 1962. Canada put a **moratorium** on the catching of northern cod that is still in effect today. Between 30,000 and 40,000 people lost their jobs when the northern cod fishery caved in. An industry that raked in $700 million each year was no more.

Today, more than 20 years after the moratorium began, the northern cod near Canada may be slowly recovering. Scientists remain cautious about lifting the fishing ban.

cod caught in a net

Bye Bye, Blue Walleye

Not every fish has had a second chance to come back. The blue walleye of the Great Lakes was overfished beginning in the 1850s. No one has seen a blue walleye since 1965, the year the last were caught. A fish can really disappear because of human actions.

The moratorium on cod fishing was only supposed to last 2 years!

BYCATCH

Many kinds of sea life are caught by mistake. Bycatch is another major factor in overfishing. It involves catching fish, crustaceans, and other sea creatures by accident.

Every fisherman deals with bycatch, even those using a simple line and hook. But commercial fishing operations contribute to bycatch in much greater numbers, especially those that have hooks and nets in the water for long periods of time. They haul in unwanted or unsellable fish that are then thrown back in the sea, sometimes dying or dead. When these creatures are already low in number, bycatch becomes a big problem.

Nontarget Species

Commercial fishermen divide fish, shellfish, and crustaceans into targets and nontargets. Targets are the ones they want. Bycatch are the unwanted nontargets. Nontargets include starfish, corals, dolphins, porpoises, sharks, sea turtles, and even seabirds. Sometimes fishermen can sell nontargets, but other times they can't for legal or business reasons.

Though this young shark was alive and released back into the water after being caught accidentally, it could have easily died or gotten hurt.

FISHING PRACTICES

Bycatch is the unavoidable result of certain fishing practices. A purse seine is a hanging net that is used to encircle fish. Fishermen gather the edges of the net and close it, like a purse. All the fish in the center of the net are then pulled into the boat. While fishermen catch schools of fish this way, they also catch whatever other creatures might be feeding on the fish.

Gill nets hang like a wall in the water. Fish run into the "wall" and get stuck. Unfortunately, so do turtles, porpoises, and other nontargets. Animals that need to swim to the surface to breathe may die in the net.

fish caught by a purse seine

Purse seines can be huge! This boat is fishing for bluefin tuna using a purse seine.

Longline Fishing

A longline uses one main fishing line, up to 50 miles (80 km) long. Smaller lines with baited hooks are tied to this line. The main line floats or is sunk, depending on the location of the target fish. However, hungry nontargets may be caught, such as turtles, sharks, and even birds.

Trawls are cone-shaped nets that are dragged in the water by moving boats. Bottom trawls are used to catch targets that are found on the ocean floor, such as rockfish and shrimp. Some people compare bottom trawls to bulldozers. They catch on reefs, rocks, and plants on the bottom of the ocean, as well as gather unfortunate amounts of bycatch.

Each year, bottom trawls disturb a seabed twice the size of the United States, often destroying habitats. Trawls dragged higher may do less damage to the seafloor, but they capture unwanted bycatch, too.

trawling net

Trawling—Frightening Facts

- One pass of a bottom trawl can remove 20 percent of plants and other habitats on the seafloor.
- Trawling bycatch includes whales, dolphins, and sea turtles, some of which are endangered.
- Shrimp trawling is the most destructive kind, accounting for one-third of all bycatch and catching just 2 percent of seafood.

Bottom trawling could be compared to bulldozing a whole rainforest while looking for one kind of plant.

▲ trawler with nets up

SOLUTIONS AND INVENTIONS

The Newfoundland cod situation has shown us what can occur if fishermen don't adopt better fishing practices. It's not too late to change. Several things need to happen, however.

First, marine scientists must find a way to calculate the populations of certain fish and then work with fishermen and governments to set up new quotas. Governments and marine protection organizations must strictly police these quotas, and fishermen must obey them. Also, the breeding grounds for endangered fish must be protected so the populations are allowed to grow. Finally, responsible fishing methods must be adopted.

MPAs

There are currently protected areas of the ocean called Marine Protected Areas, or MPAs. Fishing is either illegal or very carefully watched in these areas. Currently, MPAs cover just 1 percent of the ocean. Countries need to work together to find out which areas are in most need of the MPA label.

A police ship from the Pacific island of Palau is leading a fishing boat from Taiwan. The fishermen on board were thought to be cutting the fins off sharks, which is against the law in Palau.

Fishermen who use purse seines to catch tuna can avoid the common bycatch of dolphins by dragging the net below the surface before hauling it in, allowing the dolphins to escape over the top. Using a different kind of net may keep dolphins from getting caught as well.

A number of improvements have been suggested for trawl nets, including wider holes that would allow younger and smaller fish to swim through. Lighter materials would keep the net off the seafloor as well. Boats could also move more slowly, so certain nontarget animals can escape more easily.

TEDs

TED stands for turtle excluder device. It consists of several bars placed at the opening of a shrimp trawl and an "escape hatch." Shrimp pass though the bars, but turtles can't and are forced out of the hatch. It's now a US law for shrimp fishermen to use TEDs.

shrimp net with a bycatch-reduction device and TED

The TED is a device invented by shrimp fisherman Sinkey Boone.

25

A little knowledge of ocean life can go a long way. You might be surprised to learn that magnets **repel** sharks! This discovery led to an invention that added magnets to longlines to keep sharks away.

Another antibycatch fishing practice is the use of circle hooks on longlines. Sea turtles are less likely to swallow circle hooks and, if they do, are less likely to get snagged. Longline fishermen can also avoid certain sea creatures by weighing down lines and nets if they know the creatures swim in shallower waters or by simply steering clear of their habitats altogether.

circle hook

Cooperation

Commercial fishing companies aim to make a profit, just like any other business. Some people think the business goals are the problem. A few countries have assigned fishing rights to certain areas to just a few businesses in exchange for the businesses cooperating with each other and following rules and quotas that discourage overfishing.

Sometimes divers are able to free fish caught on the hooks from longlines.

MAKING SMART CHOICES

You can have a direct impact on the fishing industry by helping your family choose wisely at the seafood counter in your grocery store and at restaurants. Many fishermen work hard to fish in a **sustainable** way. You may see the word "sustainable" on certain products in stores and in restaurants. You can reward these fishermen for their efforts by buying sustainable seafood.

Sustainable fisheries focus on plentiful fish and those that can breed quickly. They also follow practices that reduce bycatch, obey quotas, and avoid harming habitats in other ways. If you choose seafood with the word "sustainable" next to it, you're sending a message.

Seafood = Money

When a fish, shellfish, or crustacean is in demand, businesses want to cash in. Oysters were a big business in the Chesapeake Bay for centuries but were overfished to a very low population. Besides being tasty to eat, oysters clean water, so taking them out of the bay negatively impacted the habitat's health.

The issues surrounding sustainable fishing are often in the news. You can go online to learn more about it and the sea creatures that are in danger of dying out.

CERTIFIED SUSTAINABLE SEAFOOD
MSC
www.msc.org
TM

Whole
Coho Salmon
MSC

Born/Hatc
Harvest

Glossary

algae: plantlike living things that are found mostly in water

crustacean: an animal with a hard shell, jointed limbs, feelers, and no backbone

endangered: in danger of dying out

fishery: a place where a certain kind of fish or sea creature is caught

habitat: the natural place where an animal or plant lives

moratorium: an official stopping of a certain activity for a time

overestimate: to make a guess too high

repel: to keep away

sustainable: using a natural resource in a way that doesn't harm the balance of nature

technology: the way people do something using tools and the tools that they use

trawler: a boat that drags a fishing net through water

For More Information

Books

Boudreau, Hélène. *Life in a Fishing Community.* New York, NY: Crabtree Publishing, 2010.

Stewart, Melissa. *A Place for Fish.* Atlanta, GA: Peachtree, 2011.

Websites

Ocean Portal
ocean.si.edu
Read about the many concerns scientists have about the ocean and marine life.

Overfishing
worldwildlife.org/threats/overfishing
Check out what the World Wildlife Federation has to say about overfishing.

Overfishing—A Global Disaster
overfishing.org
Find out how serious the issue of overfishing is.

Index